Playmakers

Running Backs

Tom Greve

ROURKE PUBLISHING
Vero Beach, Florida 32964

www.rourkepublishing.com

PHOTO CREDITS: © dswebb: title page, 19, 22; © Iris Nieves: page 5; © Jane Norton: 20; © Bill Grove: 6, 18; © Associated Press: 7, 12, 13, 16, 17; © brian wike: 9; © Pascal Genest: 11; © james boulette: 15; © APCortizasJr: 21

Editor: Jeanne Sturm

Cover and page design by Tara Raymo

Library of Congress Cataloging-in-Publication Data

Greve, Tom.
  Running backs / Tom Greve.
     p. cm. -- (Playmakers)
  Includes index.
  ISBN 978-1-60694-328-1 (hard cover)
  ISBN 978-1-60694-827-9 (soft cover)
  1. Running backs (Football)--United States--Juvenile literature. I. Title.
  GV951.3.G74 2009
  796.332092--dc22
                                        2009006101

Printed in the USA

CG/CG

ROURKE PUBLISHING

www.rourkepublishing.com - rourke@rourkepublishing.com
Post Office Box 643328 Vero Beach, Florida 32964

Table of Contents

Running Backs

Athletic, fast, and **durable**, running backs do most of the ball carrying for a football team's offense. They line up behind the team's **offensive line** and **quarterback,** and run toward the end zone when they get the ball. Since they run with the ball and they start from in back of the quarterback, they're called running backs.

Playmaker's FACT WITH IMPACT

*Running backs rely on their teammates on the offensive line to block **tacklers** and clear a path for them to run with the ball toward the **end zone**.*

Running backs score by carrying the ball across the goal line.

Running backs usually have the best combination of speed, balance, and durability of all the players on offense. Speed helps them outrun defensive players. Balance helps them stay on their feet and keep running when tacklers hit them. Durability allows them to keep carrying the ball time after time even though they get tackled and knocked down repeatedly.

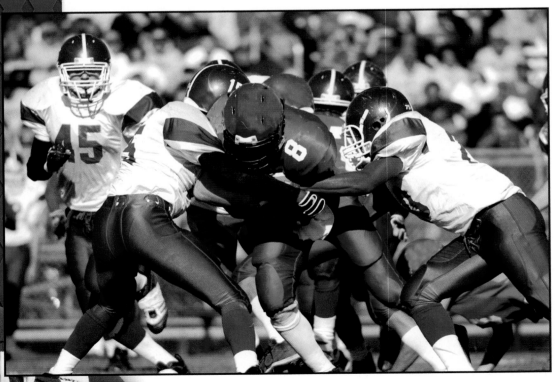

Running backs often must fight through several tacklers to try to gain extra yards without losing the ball.

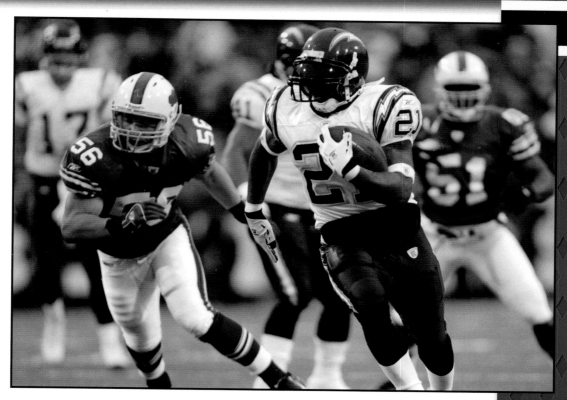

**LaDainian Tomlinson of the San Diego Chargers is
one of the best current pro running backs.**

LaDainian Tomlinson has rushed for more
than one thousand **yards** in each of his seven
professional seasons. In 2006 he scored 31
touchdowns, the most ever scored by a
player in one season, and won the league's
Most Valuable Player award. He followed that
up by leading the league in **rushing** in 2007.

Halfback Skills

There are two main running back positions. There are halfbacks, sometimes called tailbacks, who do most of the ball carrying on rushing plays. There are also fullbacks who mainly provide blocking for the halfbacks.

Playmaker's
FACT WITH IMPACT

Many college and pro offenses line up in the I-formation with the fullback in front of the halfback. In these cases, the halfback, at the tail end of the formation, is called the tailback.

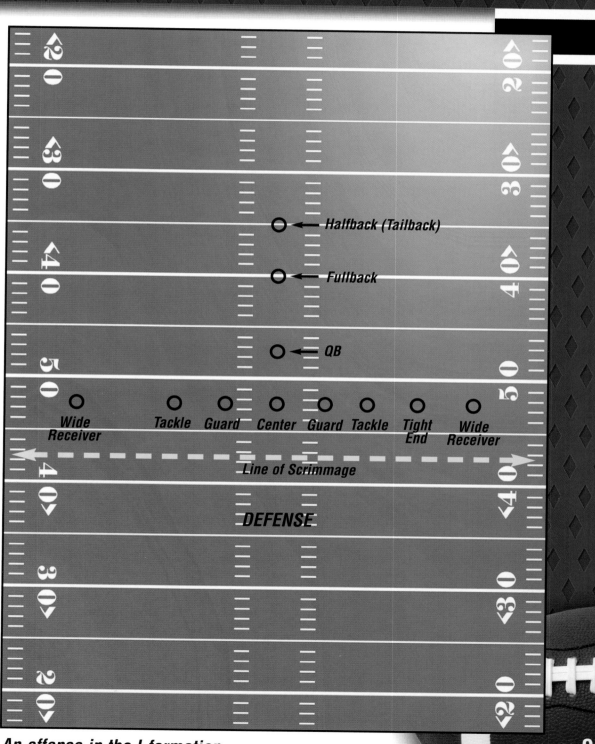

An offense in the I-formation.

The halfback often serves as the workhorse of the offense. He generally gets the most chances to run with the ball, but he also has to endure the most hits from tacklers over the course of a game.

On passing plays, the halfback helps protect the passer by blocking the defensive players or protecting against a **blitz**. He can also catch passes from the quarterback.

When defenses blitz, running backs are the last line of protection for the quarterback.

Walter Payton played for the Chicago Bears in the 1970s and '80s. He is among the greatest and most durable halfbacks in the game's history.

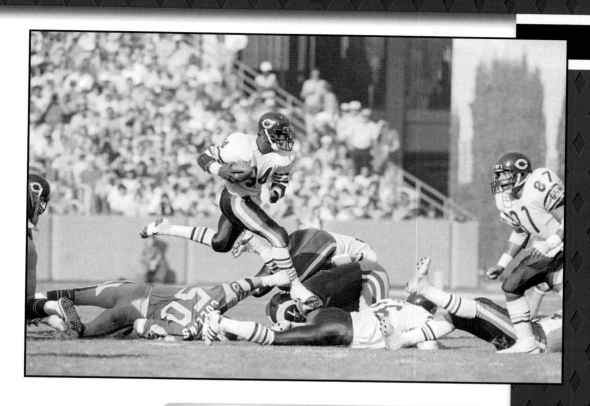

GREATS of the GAME

Walter Payton was a tough, competitive, standout athlete. His speed, strength, and ability to quickly change direction made him difficult to tackle. During his career, he broke most of pro football's rushing records. His talents as a blocker, pass receiver, and all-around performer caused his coach to call him the best football player he'd ever seen, regardless of position. He is a member of the Pro Football Hall of Fame. Sadly, Payton died of cancer in 1999.

Fullback Skills

Fullbacks, like halfbacks, have to be able to run with the ball and catch passes, but their main job is to block. They tend to be slower than halfbacks, but bigger and stronger. They specialize in blocking tacklers so the halfback can scoot past and gain yards.

Playing fullback requires vision, power, and short bursts of speed in order to locate a tackler and block him or to gain yards when carrying the ball.

Playmaker's
FACT WITH IMPACT

For college and pro teams, the fullback's role has changed in recent years. Fullbacks used to carry the ball about the same amount of time as halfbacks. Now, the fullback's role is to block. Some fullbacks might only carry the ball a few times the entire season.

Fullbacks often carry the ball in short yardage situations when a short, strong push might result in a touchdown or a **first down**.

Mike Alstott played for the Tampa Bay Buccaneers. He was among the finest fullbacks in pro football over the past 20 years.

GREATS of the GAME

Mike Alstott scored 71 touchdowns in his career as a fullback, the most by any player in Tampa Bay Buccaneer history. He was a bruising runner who always picked up tough yards when his team needed it. He was a strong lead blocker and pass receiver as well. His talent helped Tampa Bay win the Super Bowl in 2002. A neck injury forced him to retire in 2007.

So You Want to Be a Running Back?

Don't let them catch you! Running backs enjoy one of the most glorious positions on the field, but they also take a beating from tacklers on the defense. Once a running back finds room to run, he needs to be fast to outrun the defensive players to the end zone.

Hold on to that ball! Tacklers are always trying to force fumbles by knocking the ball loose from the running back.

Sometimes multiple tacklers combine to stop a running back. This is called a gang-tackle.

Practice **drills** help teach blocking techniques and skills for protecting the ball, but speed often makes the difference on the field. For high school, college, and pro players, weightlifting and exercises can also increase strength.

Coaches often have their teams run sprints on the practice field to improve the players' stamina.

Running backs practice drills like hitting the blocking sled to improve their blocking technique.

Imagine running through the woods as fast as you can, but then imagine the trees can run too, and they're trying to knock you down. That's how it is playing the position of running back.

If this sounds like fun, you might be ready to put on the pads and start learning how to be a running back!

Glossary

blitz (BLITS): an unexpected attack of the passer by one or several defensive players

drills (DRILZ): repetitive exercises that help players learn a specific skill

durable (DUR-uh-buhl): able to withstand wear and tear without slowing or breaking down

end zone (END ZOHN): the ten-yard area on each end of a football field beyond the goal line

first down (FURST DOWN): moving the ball forward 10 yards or more in four plays or less

goal line (GOHL LINE): the line teams need to cross in order to score touchdowns

offensive line (uh-FEN-siv LINE): the five blocking players who line up in front of the quarterback and running backs

quarterback (KWOR-tur-bak): passer, offensive field general

rushing (RUH-shing): running with the ball

tacklers (TAK-lurz): defensive players who knock down ball carriers

yards (YARDZ): the unit of measure most commonly used in football, one yard is equal to 3 feet or 36 inches

Index

Websites to Visit

www.nflrush.com
library.thinkquest.org/J0113128/
football.calsci.com/Positions5.html

About the Author

Tom Greve lives in Chicago with his wife, Meg, and
their two children, Madison and William. He enjoys
playing, watching, and writing about sports.